A Harper Trophy Book Harper & Row, Publishers

For Ellen right now

SOMEDAY

Library of Congress Catalog Card Number: 64-16654
ISBN 0-06-027016-0
ISBN 0-06-443207-6 (pbk.)
First Harper Trophy edition, 1989.

SOMEDAY

SOMEDAY I'm going to go to school

and everyone will say,
"How beautiful you look today. I wish I had hair like yours!"

someday

I'm going to come home
and my brother
will introduce me
to his friends and say,
"This is my sister."
Instead of
"Here's the family creep."

SOMEDAY

I'm going to go to dancing class

and Miss Bird will say,
"Ellen is doing it just right. Everybody watch her."

Someday

I'm going to catch a high, high ball

and my team will win because I did it.

I'll have one hundred dollars
and I'll buy presents
for everyone I know,
and when they thank me I'll say,

"Oh, it isn't anything. . . ."

SOMEDAY I’m going to water my plant

and find it covered with pink flowers the way it was when it first came.

SOMEDAY

my mother and father are going to say,

“Why are you going to bed so early?”

SOMEDAY

I'm going to have a little bulldog
who sleeps on my bed at night

and won't eat unless *I* feed him.

when I have nothing to read,
the doorbell will ring

and a big box of books will come for me.

SOMEDAY my mother will say to me,

“Please set the table with all the best china
for dinner tonight.
None of the everyday things.”

SOMEDAY

I'm going to be practicing the piano
and the lady across the street
will call and say,

"Please play that
beautiful piece again!"

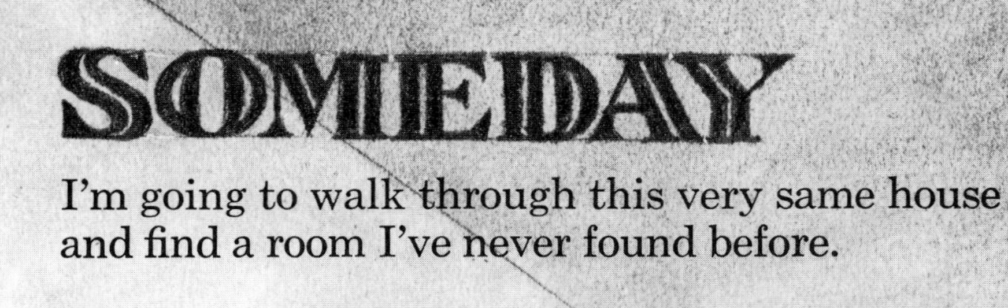

SOMEDAY

I'm going to walk through this very same house
and find a room I've never found before.

I am going to decorate the Christmas tree my own way

without my mother or my father or my brother helping.

But right now . . . it's dinnertime.